Destiny

the Pop Star Fairy

Daisy Meadows

ORCHARD

www.rainbowmagic.co.uk

The Fairyland Palace

Harwoods Department Store

The Grand Hotel

Limo

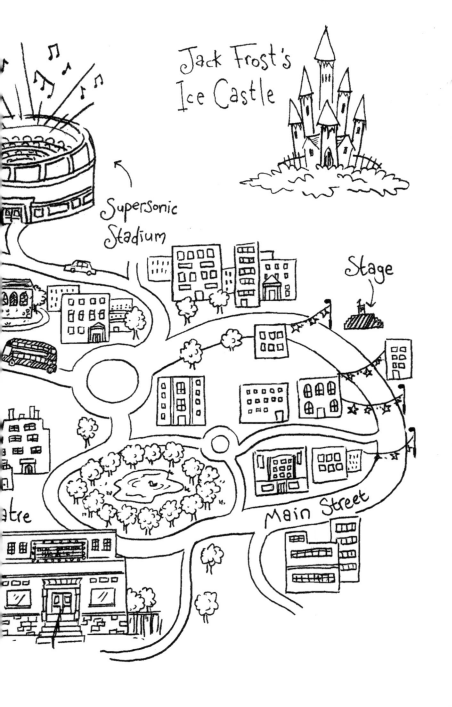

The Sparkle Sash

"I can't believe we're really going to meet Serena, Emilia and Lexy!" said Kirsty Tate to her best friend Rachel Walker. The girls had won a competition to meet their favourite band, The Angels.

The girls were staying overnight with their parents at The Grand Hotel before helping the band turn on the city's Christmas lights, and attending a charity concert. "This is almost as exciting as one of

our fairy adventures!" Rachel whispered to her best friend. No one else knew that they had a special friendship with the fairies.

"Oh, Rachel, look!" cried Kirsty. On a table in a corner of their room was a huge bunch of flowers, with a handwritten card on top. It was from the girls in the band!

Dear Kirsty and Rachel,
We hope you have a fun stay! We are really looking forward to meeting you later today. Serena, Emilia & Lexy
— The Angels xxx

"Look at the Christmas tree!"
cried Rachel, as they explored
their enormous suite. As she
spoke, there was a burst
of glitter,
and a
beautiful
fairy
appeared.

"Hello,"
she began in
a tinkling voice.
"I'm Destiny the
Pop Star Fairy, and
I need your help."

The delighted but startled girls waited for her to explain.

"I look after pop stars in the human world and Fairyland," she began. "Jack Frost wants to perform at our Christmas concert with his group, but their audition was awful! Now he's so cross he says he'll rid the world of pop music completely!"

"How could Jack Frost get rid of all music?" asked a horrified Kirsty.

"I have three magical

objects," sighed the tiny fairy.
"The Sparkle Sash protects
pop stars' outfits and costumes.
The Keepsake Key protects
their songs and music, and the
Magical Microphone ensures
the sound and lighting work
smoothly." The girls listened as
Destiny continued.

"Jack Frost has stolen them, and ordered his goblins to hide them. He wants to spoil The Angels' Christmas concert at the same time."

"But that's tomorrow!" gasped Kirsty. "What can we do to help?"

"Stay alert," said Destiny. "The goblins are bound to cause trouble sooner or later."

It was time for the girls to head for the stadium, and all thoughts of Jack Frost and goblins flew from their minds.

They were about to meet The
Angels! Arriving at the stage
door, the girls were led to the
band's dressing room. The door
opened, and The Angels rushed
over to hug them.

"Congratulations on winning the competition!" Serena said with a smile.

"It's great to meet you!" Lexy added, her copper-coloured ringlets bouncing.

"You're going to get star treatment from our own stylists," Emilia told them. "But first we're going to teach you the dance routine for our brand-new song!"

Rachel and Kirsty were giggling with The Angels like old friends as the door

14

opened. "Girls, meet Rich
and Charlotte, our stylist and
make-up artist," said Emilia.
As Charlotte dabbed glitter
onto their cheeks and eyelids,
and Rich talked about what
clothes would suit them,
Emilia's mobile phone began
to ring. Her face fell as soon

as she answered it. "But this could ruin the whole show!" she cried. Rachel and Kirsty exchanged worried looks. Could this have something to do with Jack Frost? Emilia ended the call. "The lorry carrying our costumes hasn't turned up!" she explained.

As everyone began talking at once, the girls slipped into the

corridor. A little way down,
a storage room door was open.

"Oh, no!" said Kirsty,
stepping inside.

The room was a
mess. Shimmering
costumes were
smeared with
purples, blues
and golds and
someone had used
red lipstick to draw
a picture of Jack Frost on the
wall!

"Goblins!" muttered Kirsty.

Suddenly a jet of glitter shot
from the top of a silver boot,
and Destiny appeared.

"We must find the Sparkle
Sash before the goblins cause
any more trouble!" she said,
waving her wand and clearing
the room in a flurry of magical
sparkles.

The friends followed a
horrible screeching sound to
the stage, where the goblins
were all dressed up and trying
to sing.

"Look!" Kirsty exclaimed,

pointing to
something
shimmery tied
around the
smallest goblin's
waist.

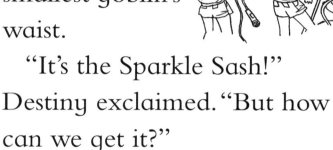

"It's the Sparkle Sash!"
Destiny exclaimed. "But how
can we get it?"

"Let's teach them The Angels'
dance routine!" smiled Kirsty.
"Then you take the sash!"

Amid the chaos of clumsily
dancing goblins, Destiny
managed to untie the sash. She

returned it to
fairy size, and
flitted away.

"Carry on
practising!"
Kirsty called out, running off
the stage.

"They've stolen my sash!"
shrieked the goblin furiously.

The disappointed goblins
shuffled off towards the exit as
Destiny waved her wand to
clear up the stage. "Thank you
so much for your help, girls,"
she said. "I could never have

got this back
without you."

"Are you
going to take
the sash back to
Fairyland now?"
asked Kirsty.

Destiny nodded.

"The sooner it's back in its
rightful place, the better!" she
declared.

Rachel and Kirsty waved
as Destiny disappeared in
a whirl of sparkles. "Come
on," whispered Rachel.

"Let's get back to The Angels!"

In the dressing room, Rachel and Kirsty found The Angels hugging and jumping around in excitement. "The lorry has been found!" Lexy squealed happily. "The driver's satnav sent him the wrong way, then the lorry broke down, then his mobile battery ran out. But just then a breakdown truck rescued him, and his satnav started working again. Can you believe it?"

"Isn't it amazing that the truck was found so quickly, and then found its way here?" said Serena to the girls.

"It's like magic!" agreed Kirsty, winking at Rachel.

Now there were only two
more magical objects left
to find!

The Keepsake Key

The next morning, Mr Tate
had a surprise for the girls. "We
thought you'd like new outfits
for the concert, so we're taking
you to Harwoods," he smiled.

"Wow!" gasped Rachel. "The
most famous department store
in the city!"

While the adults chatted, Kirsty whispered in Rachel's ear. "What about the Keepsake Key? I really want to visit Harwoods, but we must help Destiny get her other two magical objects back. Jack Frost and his goblins can't be allowed to ruin pop music forever!" But, before there was time to think, the girls were whisked off on their shopping trip.

Inside the magnificent store, Rachel and Kirsty travelled up the long escalators, feeling

very excited. The fashion
department was huge. As their
parents wandered around,
the girls hurried

eagerly
towards a
rack of
colourful,
sparkly
clothes.
"Perfect!"
said Rachel
suddenly, holding up a pretty
red skirt and distracting Kirsty.
"This would really suit you!"

"And this would look great on you," replied Kirsty, pulling out a pair of jeans with a sequin trim.

Suddenly a group of children in hooded tops pushed past them. "Hey," cried Kirsty. "Be careful!"

"It's odd to see children on their own," said Rachel thoughtfully, walking into the changing rooms.

The girls tried on their outfits, and as they were putting on their own clothes

again, Kirsty froze. Poking out
from the bottom of the next
cubicle was a pair of green feet!

"Now that is definitely a

goblin!" Rachel hissed, pulling
open the curtain. At first the
goblin inside didn't notice. He

was wearing
a purple
suit and
a striped
waistcoat.
As the
girls
watched,
he raised his
hat and admired
himself in the mirror.
Kirsty and Rachel burst out
laughing and watched the
goblin's green cheeks turn red.

"You horrible girls!" he

stammered. "How dare you laugh at me!" He stuck his tongue out at them and shot off in a rage. The girls hurried after him, but ran straight into their parents, who were waiting outside.

"Now, let's look at the shoes," said Mrs Tate, smiling.

The girls would have to give up the chase for now.

ey headed up to the
oor on the escalator, the
girls spotted three small figures
wearing wigs running up and
down, laughing and getting in
everyone's way.

"What's going on?"
a security

guard

suddenly demanded.

"Run!" shrieked a figure in a blonde wig, as he led the others towards the music department.

The girls chose their shoes quickly, then asked if they could look round on their own.

"All right," said Mrs Walker. "We'll meet you in the café."

As the girls headed off, Rachel noticed a mirror tucked away in a quiet corner, fizzing and sparkling. As she peered into it, a small figure burst through. It was Destiny! She

smiled as
she waved
her wand
and shrank
the girls to
fairy size.

"Follow me!" she
said urgently, flying towards
the electrical department. With
another sparkling wave of her
wand, The Angels appeared on
every TV screen, sitting in their
dressing room looking glum.

The girls looked confused
as Destiny explained. "The

Keepsake Key protects pop stars' songs. Every copy of the music for The Angels' new song has been stolen, and they've got to sing it tonight!"

"We're not going to let Jack Frost spoil everything," said Kirsty in a determined tone. "Come on, let's find those goblins and make them give back the Keepsake Key!"

When they reached the music department, everything seemed calm and quiet. "Have they gone?" asked Rachel.

) – listen!" said Kirsty.
The girls could hear a
squeaking sound which grew

louder and louder, until around
the corner sped a unicycle with
a squeaky wheel, ridden by
a goblin in a long silky dress.

Behind him was another on a pogo stick wearing pyjamas, and a third wobbling along on roller blades.

"Look at what that goblin on the pogo stick has around his neck," Destiny said, tingling with excitement. "It's my Keepsake Key!"

"I think I can unfasten it and fly away," Rachel whispered, ducking behind the goblin's shoulders and fluttering her wings as she tried to undo the chain.

"Something's tickling my neck!" whined the goblin, whirling around and spotting Rachel. "Look! A fairy is trying to steal the key!" He yanked the chain from around his neck and tucked it into his pyjama pocket.

"Run!" bellowed the goblin on roller blades, as they zoomed into the toy department.

There were children everywhere, but suddenly the girls heard a familiar shriek.

"Look!" Rachel exclaimed as they saw the three goblins staring in fear at a guide dog.

"Silly goblins!" said Rachel. "Guide dogs are the gentlest dogs in the world!"

Destiny giggled, but Kirsty was looking thoughtful. "Did you see those battery-powered dogs?" she whispered, smiling. "Perhaps we can distract the goblins with them!"

"That's a great idea!" smiled Destiny. She used magic to create a cloud of colourful balloons to distract the children, while the girls flitted around, shepherding the goblins closer

and closer to the yapping toy
dogs.

"Eeek!" the goblins squealed.
"Look at the hairy monsters!
Help!"

"Goblins!" said Destiny,

fluttering above them. "Please return the Keepsake Key."

"No!" squeaked the smallest goblin rudely.

At that moment one of the toy dogs yapped loudly, flipped over and landed in the lap of the goblin with the Keepsake Key. He screamed in terror, pulled the key from his pocket and threw it to Destiny, who shrank it to fairy size, catching it neatly.

"Thank you," she said, rising high into the air. "And by the way, those 'monsters' are just toys!"

"What?" roared the smallest goblin. "You tricksy fairies!"

Destiny and the girls fluttered back into the electrical department. "Thank you," the little fairy said. "I have to take the key to Fairyland but I'll be back soon. We still have to find the Magical Microphone!"

Destiny returned the girls to human size, then disappeared in a shower of glitter.

A second later, The Angels appeared on the TV screens again, laughing this time.

"Our song!" laughed Emilia. "Our music's been found!"

Soon, the Christmas lights

were due to be switched on.
Then it would be time for the
concert. Just one more magical
object to find!

The Magical Microphone

Rachel and Kirsty quickly changed, ready for the switching on of the Christmas lights and the concert.

"Come on, girls!" called Mrs Tate and, a few seconds later, the two families hurried down to the hotel lobby.

Their parents left the hotel to make their own way, while the girls rushed over to The Angels, who were waiting for them in the lobby.

"Girls, you look great!" said Serena, giving them each a hug.

"Come on, our car's here!" They led the girls out of

the hotel. A long, pink Cadillac was waiting for them, with a smart chauffeur at the wheel. Jumping in with The Angels, Rachel and Kirsty felt like pop stars themselves!

"We're really excited about turning on the lights," Emilia told them. "It's such a special occasion."

As they set off, Serena pointed at a scooter riding alongside them in the traffic. Kirsty and Rachel looked out of the window and saw six

goblins standing on the back of
it in a pyramid shape.

"Oh no!" groaned Kirsty in a
low voice. "Rachel, look at the
driver!" It was Jack Frost!

"He's got the Magical Microphone!" whispered Rachel in Kirsty's ear.

As they watched, Jack Frost roared away. The goblins held on until suddenly, the goblin at the top began to wobble and lost his balance. He fell off the scooter and landed in the middle of the road!

"Luckily everyone's wearing fancy dress for the ceremony," whispered Kirsty. "People will think he's in a costume." The girls watched as the goblin leapt to his feet, and disappeared into the crowd.

Suddenly their car began to rattle, and then stopped.

"That's not good," said Lexy as the chauffeur and The Angels got out to see what was wrong.

"Kirsty, look!" Rachel cried in excitement. The gear stick was glowing and there, on the top of it, was Destiny!

"Destiny, Jack Frost is here in the human world and we can't follow him!" Kirsty blurted

out, before the little fairy could
speak.

Destiny waved her wand and
the car roared into life.

"The car broke down
because the Magical

Microphone is missing,"
Destiny explained. "It keeps all technical things around pop stars running smoothly."

Looking relieved, The Angels and the chauffeur jumped back into the car as Destiny dived into Rachel's handbag. They arrived at the podium with seconds to spare.

Rachel and Kirsty scanned the crowd, searching for Jack Frost.

"We are thrilled," Serena said to the crowd, "to be turning on

the Christmas lights this year."

As the girls were about to
press the button, Kirsty gripped
Rachel's hand. "I see him!" she
exclaimed excitedly.

Jack Frost was standing at the edge of the crowd. Before the girls could think what to do, he stuck out his tongue, then tapped his wand against the Magical Microphone. All the lights went out, leaving Main Street in darkness. The crowd gasped.

Destiny quickly flew out of Rachel's bag. The girls didn't see her wave her wand, but felt themselves shrinking to fairy size. They all held hands together and rose into the air. The lights in the side streets were still on, and almost at once Rachel spotted a green leg disappearing through the side door of the theatre.

"This way!" she cried. Inside, the lights were down and a musical was in full swing. They split up and began to search

the theatre. Luckily it was dark
and everyone was looking at
the stage. Kirsty grabbed the
others' hands and pointed.
Jack Frost was sitting in the
back row with five goblins.
They were making so much
noise that they were disturbing

everyone around them.

"They haven't seen us," said Kirsty. "Let's creep up and try to find the Magical Microphone."

"Boo!" shouted Jack Frost rudely.

"Rubbish!" shouted one of the goblins.

"They're spoiling the show for everyone!" cried Destiny.

Just then, some stewards arrived and pinned Jack Frost's arms to his side.

"Lemme go!" wailed a goblin

as another steward seized him by the shoulders.

"I don't care how much effort you've put into these silly costumes," hissed the chief steward furiously. "We're not putting up with this noise any longer."

Jack Frost and the goblins were hauled off and thrown out of the building. Rachel quickly flew over to where they had been, and found the Magical Microphone under Jack Frost's seat! Destiny waved her wand

and returned it to fairy size.

A minute later, the three friends landed back on the podium in Main Street, next to The Angels. The street lights were back on!

"Thank you so much!" said Destiny happily. "Now I must rush to Fairyland with the Magical Microphone!" And with a sprinkle of fairy dust, she returned the girls to their normal size.

"Happy Christmas, everyone!" shouted The Angels,

Rachel and Kirsty as they
pressed the big red button
together. The Christmas lights
flashed on, and the crowd
cheered.

The concert that evening
was spectacular, and at the
end, Rachel and Kirsty went

backstage to say goodbye to
The Angels and thank them.

"I'm so sleepy!" yawned
Rachel as they changed into
their pyjamas in the hotel
room. "Oh, Kirsty – look!"

On each of their pillows was
a silver mirror, and on the back
of each was an inscription that
said, "With love and thanks,
Destiny xx". When they looked
into the glass, they could see
her waving at them, with King
Oberon and Queen Titania
behind her.

"Thank you, and goodnight!" Rachel whispered. "See you soon!"

The girls snuggled down into their beds.

"We've had lots of exciting adventures," murmured Kirsty. "But this has been the most star-studded one yet!"

The End

Reading Tips

The **National Literacy Trust** is a charity that transforms lives through literacy. We want to get more families reading. Reading is fun and children who read in their own time do better at school and later in life. By partnering with McDonald's, we hope to encourage more families to read together.

Here are some of our top tips for reading with children.

A good way to bring a book to life is to put on different voices for different characters in the story.

Why not stop at certain points in the story to ask your child what *they* think will happen next?

Setting aside some time to read with your child every day is something both of you can look forward to.

A shared love of reading can last a lifetime. You can still read aloud to your child, even when they are confident enough to read by themselves.

If your child is excited by the subject of a story, it will help keep their interest as you read together, so help them choose the books you'll read together.

ORCHARD BOOKS

This story first published in Great Britain in 2011 by Orchard Books
Early Reader edition published in 2014 by Orchard Books
This Happy Reader edition published exclusively for McDonald's in 2017 by The Watts Publishing Group

1 3 5 7 9 10 8 6 4 2

A CIP catalogue record for this book is available from the British Library.

ISBN 978 1 40835 023 2

Printed in Slovakia

MIX
Paper from
responsible sources
FSC® C104740

The paper and board used in this book are made from wood from responsible sources

Orchard Books
An imprint of Hachette Children's Group
Part of The Watts Publishing Group Limited
Carmelite House, 50 Victoria Embankment, London EC4Y 0DZ

An Hachette UK Company
www.hachette.co.uk
www.hachettechildrens.co.uk

The National Literacy Trust is a registered charity no: 1116260
and a company limited by guarantee no. 5836486 registered in England and Wales
and a registered charity in Scotland no. SC042944. Registered address:
68 South Lambeth Road, London SW8 1RL.
National Literacy Trust logo and reading tips © National Literacy Trust 2017

www.literacytrust.org.uk/donate